THERE'S A
DRAGON
IN MY
PANTS!

For my dad – T.N.

For JJ – S.H.

STRIPES PUBLISHING
An imprint of the Little Tiger Group
1 The Coda Centre, 189 Munster Road,
London SW6 6AW

A paperback original
First published in Great Britain in 2017

Text copyright © Tom Nicoll, 2017
Illustrations copyright © Sarah Horne, 2017
Author photograph © Chris Scott, 2016

ISBN: 978-1-84715-808-6

A CIP catalogue record for this book is available
from the British Library.

Printed and bound in the UK.

10 9 8 7 6 5 4 3 2 1

THERE'S A
DRAGON
IN MY
PANTS!

TOM NICOLL

ILLUSTRATED BY
SARAH HORNE

Stripes

CHAPTER 1
UNEXPECTED GUESTS

"Will you take a look at that, Eric?" said Dad, winding down his window. "It's just like I remember from when I was your age."

"It's awesome," I said, staring open-mouthed at the biggest forest I had ever seen. Beyond it was a giant pool of bright blue water. And there was the sign for the campsite:

WELCOME TO
LAKE CRESS
CAMPSITE 1 MILE

It was the end of the summer holidays and we were spending three whole nights here. Just me and my dad in the great outdoors.

A green scaly creature no bigger than a spring roll slid out of my jumper pocket and pressed itself up against my window.

"Wow, I've never seen so many trees in one place before," whispered Pan. I quickly grabbed him and put him back in my pocket before Dad could spot him.

Just me, my dad and my Mini-Dragon.

It was supposed to have only been me and my dad but the more I told Pan about how much fun the camping trip was going to be, the more he'd wanted to come. Now if you're a sensible person, you'd probably think bringing a Mini-Dragon was a bad idea. And I can see why you'd think that. But, if I know Pan, there were just two alternatives:

1. I leave him behind in the house where my mum, my little sister Posy and my cat Pusskin are having a girls' weekend. The last thing I need is for Pan to be discovered by Mum because he fancied trying one of her mud facepacks. Again. When will he listen to me — he's a Mini-Dragon, his skin is supposed to be leathery!

2. I leave him behind and he sneaks along anyway.

From past experience 2) is the likeliest option. I'd rather just let him come than find him stowed away. Trust me, I've found enough Mini-Dragons in unexpected places to last me a lifetime. Besides, when Pan's parents agreed to let him stay with me one of the conditions they made was that I showed him the world. A camping holiday in Lake Cress might not be what they had in mind but it's the best this nine-year-old can do.

As far as Dad was concerned Pan was a toy Jayden had given me for my birthday and I had no plans to change my story. So I had made Pan swear on Dragon's Honour that for the entire weekend he would obey the following rules:

No getting seen by Dad.
No getting heard by Dad.
No farting into campfires.

"Are we almost there, Mr Crisp?" asked Jayden. "I think I need a wee."

Just me, my dad, my Mini-Dragon and Jayden. Well, he is my best friend. I could hardly say no.

"Do you need a wee or do you just *think* you need a wee?" asked Min.

Just me, my dad, my Mini-Dragon, Jayden and Min. When she found out Jayden was coming, she wanted in, too. It's a good thing Dad has a family-sized tent.

"*Need*," said Jayden. "I definitely *need* a wee."

"Not far now," said Dad. "Just at the end of this track. Or I could stop right now and let you go in the woods?"

Jayden looked horrified. "Are you having a laugh?"

"Why not?" I asked. "No one's going to see you."

"You don't know that," said Jayden. "What if a bear spots me? I don't want a grizzly seeing me doing my business."

"I think you'd have bigger problems if a grizzly bear saw you," said Min. "The first thing I'd be wondering is, what was it doing here in the first place? Grizzly bears are native to North America."

"The first thing I'd be wondering is, how fast can I run away?" I said.

"Well, it wouldn't exactly be the first

creature we've known to show up in a place it doesn't come from," argued Jayden. "Maybe its parents had to smuggle it out of the country in a box of beansprouts, too."

Jayden glanced meaningfully at Pan, who was peering out of my pocket again. Pan had first come into my life when he was accidentally delivered to my house inside a takeaway dish from Min's parents' Chinese restaurant. It's a long story...

Min whistled. "That'd be one big box of beansprouts," she said. "Dad can deliver that one."

My dad laughed. "Beansprouts?" he said. "You kids have quite an imagination. Definitely no bears here – grizzly or otherwise. But look, they do have a toilet block."

"Good," said Jayden, jigging around in his seat. I knew he must be desperate as he didn't seem bothered that the toilets looked like they were falling apart.

The car came to a stop and Jayden flung open his door and sprinted towards the toilet block. The rest of us got out and stretched our legs. Pan was equally keen to stretch his tail, hopping out of my pocket as soon as he got the chance. Before Dad could see him, I grabbed the Mini-Dragon and slipped him back.

"Wow," whispered Pan, taking in the campsite. "The last time I saw anything as green as this I was looking in a mirror."

Already I was thinking about where we should pitch our tent. But then I realized something was missing.

"Where is everyone?" asked Jayden as he returned, looking a lot more comfortable.

Dad frowned. "Hmm. Not very busy is it? Maybe we're early."

Min looked at her watch. "It's half three."

"The site manager said there were definitely going to be some other people here," said Dad, looking around. Then something seemed to occur to him. "Of course, how could I forget? There's another site across the lake where the older types go – birdwatchers and photographers mostly. This side used to be packed with families. Strange it's not so popular now. I guess people prefer to go abroad these days." He let out a sigh. "I guess we could move..."

"No way," I said. "We've got an entire campsite to ourselves. It's brilliant."

"You're right," Dad said. "Who wants to hang out with birdwatchers anyway? But about having the campsite to ourselves—"

HONK-HONK!

We turned round as a white Porsche roared into the clearing, screeching to a stop beside us. A blacked-out passenger window rolled down and a scowling, red-faced boy stuck his head out.

"Is this it, Crispo?" sneered Toby, my next-door neighbour/mortal enemy, looking around. "Is this what you've been banging on about for weeks? Some trees?"

I turned to my dad, unable to find the words.

Jayden found them for me. "Why is Toby here?" he asked.

Dad looked at us apologetically. "Oh … well … I might have … kind of … invited him."

"YOU WHAT?" I shouted, so loud that birds scattered from the trees.

"Eric, keep your voice down," said Dad. "I was chatting to Frank the other day and I mentioned our trip, and he said that he'd love to get away with Toby. Before I knew it, somehow I'd managed to invite them along. I didn't think they'd actually come, though. Frank's always working."

I sighed.

Just me, my dad, my Mini-Dragon, Jayden, Min, and Frank and Toby Bloom.

CHAPTER 2
THERE GOES THE NEIGHBOURHOOD

"Ah, Monty, you're here already," said Toby's dad as he got out of the car. "We would have beaten you but Toby spotted a Chick-a-Licious Express and insisted we stop for a quick bucket of wings."

Dad smiled politely. "Glad you could make it."

"I'm not," came a voice from my pocket.

"Shh, Pan," I said.

Toby didn't bother getting out of the car. He had already turned back to the tablet he was holding.

"You coming, son?" asked Mr Bloom.

"Watching my show," grunted Toby.

Mr Bloom laughed heartily. "It's that *Inspector Dragon* series. He's obsessed with dragons these days."

Pan and I exchanged nervous glances. After multiple attempts by Toby to get his hands on Pan, we knew only too well how obsessed with dragons he was.

"Well, why don't we get the tents set up?" said Dad.

"Yeah!" I said, eager to move the conversation away from dragons.

Mr Bloom didn't seem to hear Dad. Instead he was waving his phone around as if he was trying to swat a fly.

"What's the story with the phone signal, Monty?" he asked. "Not even getting a bar. Said I'd check in with Mrs Bloom when I arrived."

"You won't get a signal here," said Dad. "That's what's so great about this place. Getting back to nature, without all our gadgets."

Mr Bloom nodded and continued to wave his phone about. He pointed towards the track we had just driven down. "Think I'll try over there," he said, walking off.

"We can still get started with our tent," Dad said. "Toby, would you like to help?"

Toby mumbled something. None of us could quite make it out but from the way he then rolled up the car window his answer must have been "No".

"So, where's the instructions?" asked Jayden, once Dad had laid out the contents of the tent bag in front of us.

"Oh, long gone," Dad said. "This was Eric's grandad's tent. And no one tells Grandad Crisp what to do."

"Except for Gran," I added.

Dad laughed. "Well, apart from Gran."

"What's this then?" asked Min, picking up a dusty old booklet that was lying among the pegs. She wiped it clean, revealing a yellowy cover. *"Lake Cress Guidebook '79."*

"Ah, I forgot we had that," said Dad. "Everything you ever wanted to know about the area, you could find in there. So long as it happened before the eighties."

Min flicked through it for a few moments before slipping it into her back pocket.

"Right then," said Dad. "I'm sure we can figure this thing out. How hard can it be?"
Answer: quite hard, as it turns out.

After about twenty minutes we stood back and admired our tent.

Admired might be the wrong word. As might tent...

The tent looked as if it was standing up more by chance than anything else. The poles holding it in place wobbled nervously as though all it would take to bring the whole thing down would be a slight breeze. Or for someone to look at it the wrong way.

"Are we really going to sleep in that?" asked Min.

Dad stroked his beard. "Hmm. I'll check in the car and see if I have any more rope we can use to secure it."

As soon as Dad was out of sight, Pan leaped down from my pocket.

"I can see that this is going to need a Mini-Dragon's touch," he said.

"I suppose you're going to tell us that

Mini-Dragons are excellent at putting up tents," said Jayden.

Pan shrugged. "No idea," he said. "Never tried. Couldn't possibly be worse than you lot, though."

"He's got a point," I said. "Be our guest, Pan."

"OK, you three hold it up for me," he said, cracking his claws and diving into action.

He moved so fast that he was nothing more than a blur as he dug the pegs out of the ground. Min, Jayden and I grabbed the tent to stop it from collapsing altogether, as the ropes holding it up slackened. Then Pan disappeared beneath the canvas and all we could hear was the metallic clinking of tent poles being rearranged. Finally he emerged from the tent and proceeded to tighten the guy ropes, stomping up and down on the pegs like a tiny pneumatic drill.

"Done," said Pan.

It looked great. Like an actual tent, which certainly hadn't been the case five minutes ago.

"OK, I'll admit it," said Jayden. "Mini-Dragons are excellent at putting up tents."

"Better than us, that's for sure," I said. "Thanks, Pan."

"Look, it even has a door now," said Min. "I was wondering where that was."

I heard the car boot slam shut and turned round to see Dad making his way back towards us. I put Pan back in my pocket.

"I looked everywhere but I couldn't find any rope," said Dad. "However, I do have this roll of medical tape from my first-aid kit. Maybe I could use it to—"

Dad's mouth fell open as he saw the tent. "You ... fixed it?"

As I struggled to think of an explanation, Min beat me to it.

"It actually wasn't as bad as it looked, Mr Crisp," she said. "It just needed a few minor adjustments."

"Ah ... OK," said Dad, still looking a bit confused. He opened up the zip and peered inside. "Wow, much better! Thank you, everyone."

By this time Mr Bloom had reappeared, along with Toby.

"Nice tent, Monty," said Mr Bloom, giving Toby a wink.

"Oh, thanks, Frank," said Dad, tossing the medical tape into the tent. "Did you find a signal then?"

Mr Bloom frowned and shook his head. "It's all these trees. If you ask me, someone needs to chop down a few and put up a decent phone mast. Not to worry, though, there's a phone box about half a mile up the road."

"Great," said Dad. "Do you want us to help you with your tent?"

"That won't be necessary," said Mr Bloom. "It's all in hand. In fact, I think this is us now."

We all turned as a loud roar filled the campsite and a large truck pulled into the clearing.

On its side were the words:

HAPPY GLAMPERS

The truck came to a stop and three burly men dressed in bright red uniforms got out. One of them approached us, carrying a hand-held signature pad.

"Bloom?" he grunted.

"That's me," said Mr Bloom.

"Sign here please," said the man. He then whistled at the other guys, who opened the back of the truck and began removing lots of heavy-looking boxes.

Toby had that smile on his face. You know the one I mean. The one he has whenever he's about to show me something he has that I don't.

"Wait till you see what a real tent looks like, Crispo," he said.

CHAPTER 3
KEEPING UP WITH THE BLOOMS

It took the men hardly any time at all to assemble the tent. If you could even call it a tent. As the truck drove off everyone stood gazing at the *thing* in wonder.

"Have you ever seen a tent like it?" boomed Mr Bloom.

"I can honestly say I haven't," said Dad.

OK, how to describe it? Well, the most obvious thing is that it was big. And not just big for a tent. I've seen smaller houses. It was a good job that the campsite was so quiet. With even a few more tents around there wouldn't have been space for Castle Bloom at all.

"It's got ten rooms," said Mr Bloom. "Six bedrooms with en-suite bathrooms, a living room, a kitchen, a dining room…"

"And a games room!" blurted out Toby, pushing past his dad and disappearing through the flap.

Moments later we could hear explosions coming from inside.

"I hope that's just a video game," laughed Mr Bloom, "or I won't be getting my deposit back. So, Monty, what do you think?"

I could see my dad trying to think of a polite answer. "Well ... I mean ... it's a bit big, isn't it?"

"Course it's big," said Mr Bloom. "Blooms don't do small. Go big or go home, that's what I always say."

"Wish they would go home," whispered Pan.

"Me, too," I said.

Dad looked at me, confused. "I've never heard you say 'Go big or go home' before, Eric," he said.

"What? Oh, no, I meant..." I stammered.

"Smart kid you've got there, Monty," said Mr Bloom, slapping me on the back. "I can see why Toby looks up to him so much."

"NO, I DON'T, DAD!" shouted Toby from inside the tent.

"He does really," whispered Mr Bloom, giving me a wink. "Anyway, are we going to stand about all day gawping or are we actually going to do something fun?"

Dad perked up at this. "You're right,

Frank," he said. "I was thinking we could start by catching some fish in the lake for dinner. Then we could build a campfire to cook them on."

Mr Bloom looked at Dad as if Dad had just told a joke he didn't understand the punchline to. "Suuuuure..." Mr Bloom said slowly. "We could do. Or we could just use the cooker back there and all the food that Happy Glampers have provided. You want fish, Monty? There's a freezer full of the things. Now, when I said something fun, I meant we could watch the latest Slug Man movie on the 50-inch 3-D TV in the living room. And I know what you're thinking – yes, there are enough glasses for everyone."

I rolled my eyes. As if we were going to waste our weekend sitting in front of a television.

"Yeah, let's do that!" said Jayden.

"Do you have the extended edition?" asked Min.

"Of course," said Mr Bloom.

"Count me in," she said.

Dad looked at me. "And you, Eric?"

I was about to say no way when I looked down at Pan, who was nodding eagerly.

And then I remembered that I haven't actually seen the extended version.

"Maybe just one film," I said. "And then we can do those other things?"

Dad sighed but nodded.

Three movies later...

"Right," I said, getting up off the fancy leather couch. "Three Slug Man films is probably enough. Besides, the next one is rubbish. Do you want to do something outside now, Dad? Dad?"

I looked over at Dad, who had nodded off in one of the armchairs.

"Dad," I said, giving him a nudge. "The films are over now, if you still want to do something."

Dad opened his eyes and let out a yawn. He checked his watch then pulled back the curtain to peer out of the window. "Not tonight, Eric. It's late and it's been a long day. We should probably think about turning in."

"All right," I said. I glanced over at Min and Jayden. "You two coming?"

Min and Jayden looked awkwardly at each other.

"Actually, mate," said Jayden. "We were thinking ... if Mr Bloom doesn't mind ... it's just ... the sleeping compartments here look a lot bigger..."

"This way everyone will have more space," said Min.

Mr Bloom laughed. "The more the merrier," he said. "And there's two more rooms if you guys want them?"

"No, thank you," I said. "We'll sleep in *our* tent."

I made sure to scowl at Jayden and Min on the way out, although both did their best not to look at me.

It was only when Dad and I actually got inside our tent that it hit me how small it was. It had two zipped-off sections on either side of a middle living area but once all our bags were inside there wasn't much space left. Even though there was no way I was going to admit it, it was probably a good thing that Min and Jayden were sleeping in the Blooms' tent. But as we unpacked our sleeping bags by torchlight I could tell my dad was a bit disappointed with how things had gone so far, too.

"Night, Eric," he said.

"Night, Dad," I said back.

I thought I should say something else. Tell him that tomorrow we'd fit in so much outdoorsy stuff that we'd forget there even was an inside. But before I could find the words, I heard him snoring.

"Oh no," said Pan, climbing out of my pocket. "I forgot how loud your dad snores."

"Look who's talking," I said.

Pan looked outraged. "How dare you! Mini-Dragons are excellent at not snoring."

"Ha!" I said. "Listen, Pan, tomorrow we need to make sure Dad has a better time than he did today. He's been looking forward to this trip for just as long as we have."

"No problem," he said. "Besides, I had a flick through the rest of the Blooms' movie collection. They don't have very good taste, you know."

"That's not exactly news," I said. "Wait, when did you sneak out?"

"When you were all in the dining room eating burgers," said Pan. "It's a good job Min brought some prawn crackers, by the way. I don't like the look of camping food. Hey, do you think there might be any mountain goats around here?"

Mountain goats and prawn crackers are two of the three main Mini-Dragon food groups. The other being dirty washing.

"I don't think so, Pan," I said. "Anyway, you need to be careful. The last thing we need is for you to be spotted by someone like Mr Bloom."

Pan waved dismissively. "If he's like his son, he'll just think I'm a high-tech toy."

"Yeah, well, there's Dad, too," I said. "Now let's get some sleep. Oh, wait, I almost forgot."

I reached into my backpack for the tiny sleeping bag I had found for Pan. I couldn't believe my luck when I'd come across it among my old toys. It was an accessory from an Army Man figurine. It was just the right size for a Mini-Dragon. It was perfect. It was...

...not there.

"Pan, did you remember to pack that sleeping bag I gave you?" I asked.

"Me? You said *you* were going to pack it," said Pan.

"No..." I said, before my voice trailed off. "Oh, wait, I did say that, didn't I?"

"You forgot it?" groaned Pan. "Now where am I going to sleep?"

I fumbled in my bag, trying to find something. I pulled out clothes, socks, all those pairs of pants that Mum had made me bring "just in case" and our walkie-talkies, which I'd figured might be useful in an emergency. "Nothing here, I'm afraid," I said, shaking out the now-empty bag.

Pan disagreed. "These'll do," he said. He was holding up a pair of my underpants.

"Those are my pants," I said.

Pan sniffed them. "Clean?" he asked.

"Of course they are," I said, a little insulted he would even ask.

"Then they're perfect," he said.

No one had ever called my pants that before.

"Pan, I really don't see how…"

But Pan wasn't listening. He opened the zip of our compartment a little and jumped out.

"Where are you going?" I hissed.

Seconds later he was back, carrying Dad's medical tape.

With his razor-sharp claws, Pan sliced off a couple of pieces of tape and stuck them on either end of my pants, before fixing them to the corner of the tent making—

"A pants hammock," I said.

Pan hopped in. "Now this is comfy," he said, stretching out.

I shook my head as I shoved all my stuff back into my bag. I suppose it was lucky that Mum had made me bring spare pants or else I'd have to wear a pair inside out for a day. Gross.

"So when are we going to work on my flying, by the way?" said Pan, stifling a yawn.

I groaned. I had completely forgotten about that. One of the other conditions Pan's parents had for letting him stay was that I helped him learn to fly. Pan's flying was not much better than mine. I had promised we'd do some training this weekend but I wasn't looking forward to it.

"If you wake me first thing, we can head out before everyone else gets up," I said, climbing into my sleeping bag. "Goodnight, Pan."

"Goodnight, Eric."

CHAPTER 4
HOW TO TRAIN YOUR MINI-DRAGON

It was just after eleven when I finally emerged from my tent, hair sticking to my head from sweat. I winced as the sunlight caught my eyes.

"Morning," said Jayden with a smirk. He was sitting next to Min at a wooden table outside the Blooms' tent. In front of them were plates full of sausages, bacon, fried eggs, baked beans, mushrooms, tomatoes and toast. It smelled amazing. Jayden handed me an empty plate, which I quickly filled.

"Wow, you look terrible," said Min.

"Gee thanks, Min," I said, slumping down in a chair.

"Rough night?" she asked.

I nodded. "At some point Pan and Dad's snoring synchronized so that one was breathing out while the other was breathing in. Just one long, never-ending snore. Hey, wait a minute, where is Pan?"

Min pointed at her welly. Pan was tucked inside, eating some prawn crackers.

"Oh, Pan," sighed Min. "I said to be careful. You're getting crumbs inside my boot."

"Sorry, Min," said Pan. "Morning, Eric."

I checked my watch. "Why didn't you wake me?" I muttered. "I said I wanted to be up early."

"I tried," said Pan. "But you told me to go away."

It all started coming back to me now...

I wasn't very polite about it, either.

"Sorry," I said. "I was just tired. And it didn't help that I couldn't get comfortable. I swear we must have pitched the tent on a rockery or something."

"Well, I slept great," said Pan. "Eric, if you don't mind me saying, your underpants are extremely comfortable."

Min and Jayden gave me an odd look so I explained about the hammock.

"You could have slept in our tent," said Min. "It's got proper beds and everything."

"Oh, it's *your* tent now, is it?" I said. "That's funny, because I thought it was Toby and his dad's tent."

"You know what I mean," said Min. "Stop being so grumpy."

I took a bite of toast and the four of us went without speaking for a few minutes.

"Hey, Min," said Jayden, breaking the silence. "Tell Eric about the legends of Lake Cress."

"The what?" I said.

"It's in the guidebook," she said. "There are tons of local legends. Obviously none of them are real. They're probably just made up to attract tourists."

I looked around at the empty campsite. "Doing a great job," I said. "Go on then, let's hear some of them."

Min picked out her top five:

Min's Top Five Probably-Not-True Lake Cress Stories

1. Bigfoot was originally from the area but emigrated to America on the *Mayflower* in 1620. It was able to blend in on board because people were much hairier in those days.

2. Alien abductions are so regular in Lake Cress that many of the locals have started using them as a free taxi service.

3. Elvis himself lives in the woods and can sometimes be heard howling at the moon like a hound dog. But don't you step on his blue suede hiking boots. He doesn't like that.

4. The Lady of the Lake — keeper of Excalibur, the sword of King Arthur — often spends her summers here. Lake Cress is one of the deepest lakes in the world, so it's best if you don't go looking for her.

5. Robin Hood actually lived here and NOT Sherwood Forest but it'd be too expensive to have to change all the books, so they keep it as it is.

"Ooh, there's another one here about a golden tooth—" said Min.

"Where is everyone anyway?" I interrupted.

"Toby's playing video games," said Jayden. "His dad's watching some American box set about a psychic plumber who solves crimes and your dad's just gone off to find that phone box."

Pan clambered out of Min's welly and into mine. "Now might be a good time for some flying practice," he said.

"Sure." I nodded. I was planning to find somewhere nearby that was suitably hidden, which hopefully wouldn't be too difficult to do in a forest. If we left right away, we could fit in a quick session and maybe even be back before Dad, leaving us the rest of the day to do proper camping stuff. I looked at Min and Jayden. "You two ready to go?"

The pair of them exchanged awkward glances. "Er … actually, mate…" said Jayden.

"…we kind of agreed to a table-tennis match against the Blooms," continued Min.

I was close to exploding. "Table tennis?" I said. "You're telling me they have space for a table-tennis table in there?"

Jayden nodded. "Only just," he said. "I mean, you have to move the pool table right to the back of the room to make it fit."

I shook my head in disbelief. "Fine," I said, standing up. "Enjoy your game. Come on, Pan."

I had only taken a few steps when Min cried out, "Eric, wait!"

I stopped. I knew my friends weren't really going to abandon us for ping pong with the Blooms.

"Yes?" I said.

"Aren't you going to get washed first?" she sighed.

I skipped the wash and headed off with Pan into the woods. After walking for about ten minutes along a dirt path near the lake we found a clearing that seemed ideal.

Pan slipped out of my welly and stretched his wings.

"Can you believe Min and Jayden?" I said.

Pan shook his head. "I know. Why would anyone want to play table tennis when they could be helping me learn to fly?"

I remembered how badly Pan's previous flying lessons had gone and suddenly found myself less mad with my friends. Table tennis was definitely more fun, even if it did involve Toby. It was safer, too.

The first time I ever saw Pan try to fly, he almost destroyed my bedroom. It was only recently, after his parents asked me to help teach him, that I saw Pan fly again. The second time we decided to move it outdoors and he almost destroyed my back garden. The time after that we found a secluded area of Bramble Park and he actually did destroy an old shed. I had been tracking our results so far and they weren't pretty:

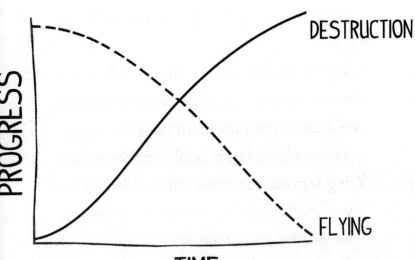

PROGRESS

DESTRUCTION

FLYING

TIME

"Today's the day," he said. "I can feel it."

"You say that every time." I sighed. "If you can just avoid knocking down any trees, I think you'll be doing well."

Pan folded his arms. "It wouldn't kill you to be a bit more encouraging, you know."

"You're right," I said. "Sorry. OK, today's the day then. Let's start with our drills. Wings to the side."

This was a strategy I had borrowed from hearing Dad talk about the training he puts his football team, the Kippers, through every week. The idea was to break flying down into a few manageable activities that Pan could focus on one at a time. Hey, if it's good enough for the Kippers... Oh, right, yeah, the Kippers are still rubbish. Well, it was worth a try anyway.

Pan extended his leathery wings.

"And flap-two-three-four," I said as Pan began moving his wings up and down.

"Flap-two-three-four," I repeated. "And faster-two-three-four."

Pan began to flap harder and harder as I repeated the drills.

"And jump," I said.

Pan leaped up, flapping furiously. He managed to stay airborne for a few seconds before dropping back down.

"Come on, Pan, you can do it," I said. "Keep flapping. One, two, three – jump!"

Pan jumped again, and this time actually started to rise a little in the air, climbing as high as my head before slowly falling to the ground. It was a great effort – his best so far.

"That was brilliant, Pan. You had it there!" I cheered.

"I think I need a rest," he panted.

"No, don't stop now," I said. "Come on, one more go. One, two, three – jump."

A steely look of determination filled Pan's face as he balled up his claws, clenched his teeth and sprang into the air. He soared above my head. It was glorious. It was breathtaking. It was ... a complete disaster.

Pan was too excited to notice the tree. He must have been about twenty metres off the ground, busy smiling and waving at me, when he smacked his head on a branch. There was a loud crack as the wood almost snapped in half, and a shower of leaves rained down on me. The collision knocked him off course and he began ricocheting off tree after tree. It reminded me of his flight attempt the first night I met him where he bounced off everything in my room. Except this time he had an entire forest to whack into.

I chased him through the trees, trying my best to shout words of encouragement as his little green head bounced around like a pinball but it was no use. It was only when he reached the edge of the forest that the ordeal finally came to an end.

Well, almost. He might have run out of trees but there was plenty of water. Pan shot out over Lake Cress, skimming across the surface like a pebble before finally disappearing into the deep water.

I realized then that I had no idea if Pan could swim. The closest I had seen to him swimming had been when his Aunt Maria and Uncle Fernando tried to dragon-nap him using our toilet. Luckily I'd managed to stop them thanks to some fine plunging work but

I never actually found out if Pan was able to swim by himself.

As I gazed out across the lake, the signs weren't good. Pan was nowhere to be seen. I had no choice. I shook off my wellies and dived into the water. I was finally grateful for all those hours our PE teacher Mr Gunnar had spent ~~shouting at~~ ~~yelling at~~ ~~screaming at~~ teaching us to swim.

I swam as fast as I could towards the middle of the lake. On the far bank I could make out the other campsite Dad had mentioned. I wondered if any of the campers were looking out on to the lake right then, asking themselves what a nine-year-old boy was doing going for a dip in the freezing-cold water.

I was so busy trying to fight through the cold that I didn't even notice the tiny green creature heading towards me.

"Hey, Eric," said Pan as he casually swam past.

"H-h-hey, P-P-Pan," I said, my teeth chattering as I spoke.

"Where are you going?" he called.

"T-t-to s-s-save y-y-you," I called back.

I swam another few metres before it hit me. I stopped and turned round.

Well, at least I got that wash.

CHAPTER 5
THERE'S A DRAGON IN MY GENERATOR!

"Are you sure you're all right?" I asked Pan as we walked back to camp, dripping water as we went. "You took some pretty bad knocks back there."

"I'm fine," said Pan, waving me away. "Mini-Dragons are tough."

"So are trees," I said.

"Not as tough as Mini-Dragons," said Pan. "We're very thick-skinned. You need to be when you grow up in a cave. I must have banged my head on a rock at least once a day."

"That explains a lot," I said.

Pan didn't look too amused. "Very funny," he said.

"Oh, come on." I laughed. "I thought you had a thick skin... Hey, hang on, are we going the right way?"

The two of us stopped and looked around. We should have reached our tent by now. Instead all we could see were more trees.

Pan pointed behind us. "Aren't we camped back that way?" he asked.

"I'm not sure," I said. "The lake's over there, so... Wait, can you hear that?"

Pan tilted his head to hear better and nodded. It was hard to make out but it sounded like someone talking.

"Come on," I said, picking up Pan. I followed the voice through the trees. Maybe I could ask whoever it was for directions.

Then the main road came into view and I

knew I wouldn't need to bother. I just had to follow it back to camp.

"I'm telling you, Maya, it's a bit of a washout to be honest."

I froze.

"Isn't that your—" began Pan, before I covered his mouth with my hand.

It was Dad. I ducked behind a tree. He was standing at a phone box about ten metres away, talking to Mum.

"The kids don't seem that interested," Dad continued. "They spent most of yesterday watching movies on Frank's giant TV. And it looks like today will be more of the same. Eric? He was still asleep last I checked. Yeah, maybe we'll do something. I don't know…"

"Wow," whispered Pan. "Your dad doesn't sound happy."

"Of course he isn't," I said. "The Blooms are ruining everything as always. Well, that's it. We're going to put an end to this."

"NOOOOO!" cried Toby.
"NOOOOOOO!" cried Mr Bloom.
Seconds later a panicked Toby and Mr Bloom emerged from their tent. With Pan safely tucked inside my welly, I walked towards them as if I was just coming back from the lake. As I reached their tent, my

dad appeared from the opposite side.

"What's up?" asked Dad, looking at me. "And why are you soaking?"

"I … er … went for a swim," I said.

"The electricity's out," explained Jayden as he and Min appeared behind the Blooms.

"Oh?" I said innocently. "How did that happen?"

"I don't know," said a pale-faced Mr Bloom. "But I intend to find out."

We followed him round to the large red generator that had been providing all the power. Mr Bloom took one look at it before holding his head in his hands.

"What is it, Dad?" asked Toby. "Can you fix it?"

"I'm afraid not, son," Mr Bloom said. "It looks like something's been chewing at the wires. Maybe a rat. I'd better move everything out of the freezer…"

Min and Jayden's heads turned towards me. I looked away but I could still feel their suspicion burning holes through me.

"Can't you just get the company to come and fix it?" asked a desperate Toby.

"They only do emergency call-outs for platinum-level customers," said Mr Bloom. "We're gold level. It's 48 hours for us. We'll be off home by then."

"We're only gold level?" wailed Toby. "You're so cheap!"

Mr Bloom put his hand on his son's shoulder. "Now, Toby, I'm just as upset as you are by this. I still had loads of box sets to get through. But I'm afraid we won't be getting the electricity back on."

Toby flung himself to the ground, sobbing inconsolably.

"Oh dear," said my dad. I could see him trying to hide a smile as he added, "Well, that is a shame."

"Dad, can we stop at that chicken place on the way home?" asked Toby, getting back to his feet and wiping his snotty nose on his sleeve.

Mr Bloom looked confused. "On Monday? Sure," he said.

Toby's eyes almost popped out of their sockets. "Monday?" he said. "You can't seriously be suggesting we're going to stay here? You just said the electricity won't be coming back on."

"Yes... but—" began Mr Bloom.

"There are plenty of fun things we can do without electricity, Toby," interrupted Dad. "You wait and see. On Monday, you won't want to go home."

"You're right, I don't want to go home on Monday," said Toby. "I want to go home now."

"Honestly, Toby," I said. "It's going to be great. Dad's brilliant at outdoor stuff. No one's better."

Er ... wait a minute, why was I trying to convince Toby to stay?

Dad blushed a little. "You're exaggerating, Eric," he said. "But I do think that—"

Toby's face turned dark. "My dad's better," he snapped.

"What?" I said.

"You heard me, Crispo," said Toby. "The

only reason you think your dad's any good is that you've never seen my dad in action."

"Now, Toby," said Mr Bloom, laughing nervously, "I don't think…"

I could feel my blood boiling. "I know you're upset about not getting to play your video games," I said. "But we all know that's not true."

"Yes, it is. My dad earns about a hundred times what your dad earns," said Toby. "So he'd be a hundred times better at anything your dad can do. That's just maths."

I snapped. "All right then," I said. "If your dad's so good at outdoors stuff, how about a challenge?"

"You're on!" shouted Toby.

Dad laughed. "Come on now, Eric, we're not going to have a contest. Right, Frank?"

Mr Bloom seemed to be giving the idea some thought. He turned to Toby. "You really think your old man can win?" he asked.

"You'll crush him, Dad," said Toby. "Just like everyone crushes his rubbish football team every week."

Mr Bloom grinned. "How about it, Monty? I mean, unless you're scared you'll lose?"

"What? No, of course not. I just meant..." said Dad, sounding flustered. He glanced over at me as I nodded at him encouragingly. Then his face took on a look of determination. "OK, Frank. You're on."

I was too caught up in the argument to notice Min and Jayden sidling up next to me.

"Hope you know what you're doing," whispered Jayden.

Min, meanwhile, was staring down at Pan. "Must be some smart rats they have out here," she said. "Smart enough to switch the power off on the generator before they start messing around with it."

Pan and I exchanged guilty looks.

"Yeah, they must be really smart," I agreed.

CHAPTER 6
GONE FISHING

There were to be three challenges. Dad got to choose one and Mr Bloom the other. The third was to be chosen by the judges – Min and Jayden.

"You can't put those two in charge," protested Toby. "They're Eric's friends – no way they'll be fair."

Jayden pretended to look hurt. "What do you mean?" he said.

"If it makes you feel better, Toby, I think both sides are being just as ridiculous as each other," said Min.

"It's fine, son," said Mr Bloom. "It's just a friendly competition ... that we're totally going to win."

As Toby's face filled with glee, the games got under way.

After winning a coin toss, Mr Bloom got to choose the first event – fishing.

It seemed like an odd choice for Mr Bloom. After shooting down the idea yesterday, I would never have pegged him as a fisherman.

"Just to warn you, Monty," said Mr Bloom as we reached the banks of Lake Cress. "I'm a bit of a dab hand at fishing. Comes from years of practice on business weekends."

"What's fishing got to do with business?" asked Jayden.

"Oh, only everything," said Mr Bloom, giving him a knowing smile. "I often take clients out on the yacht. Cast your reel and seal the deal, that's what I always say. Anyway, shall we get started?"

"Sure," said Dad as he finished putting together his fishing rod. To be honest, it wasn't much more than a bit of string on a pole. Not like Mr Bloom's rod, which was long, sleek and black, with little white fish skeletons painted up the side.

"The Super-Caster 3000," he said, holding up the rod.

Dad didn't look very confident. I smiled and gave him the thumbs up, even though I couldn't help thinking his chances of winning were about the same as Pan's chances of being able to fly back home.

"Right," said Jayden. "The winner is the first to catch three fish. Contenders ready? Three... Two... One... Go!"

"Wow, this is boring," said Pan. He wasn't wrong.

It was almost an hour later and neither my dad nor Toby's had caught a thing. Well, actually, that's not quite true. Between them, they had caught:

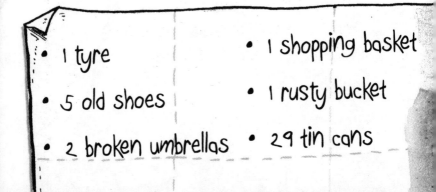

- 1 tyre
- 5 old shoes
- 2 broken umbrellas
- 1 shopping basket
- 1 rusty bucket
- 29 tin cans

Pan and I had almost drifted off a few times, and Jayden had fallen asleep ages ago. Min was still awake but she'd given up watching and was flipping through the guidebook instead. Only Toby seemed genuinely gripped by the whole thing, convinced that any minute now his dad was going to win.

"I think I've got something," said Dad suddenly as his line began to jerk.

"Probably another tin can," whispered Pan.

But this time it wasn't. "It's a fish!" cried Dad, reeling it in. "Look at the size of it. It's a monster!"

Well, it was a fish. But it was no monster. In fact, it was smaller than Pan.

Min gave Jayden a nudge.

"Huh ... what?" said Jayden, wiping dribble from his chin. "Oh ... they're *still* going."

"We have our first fish," said Min. "Mr Crisp leads one–nil."

"Yes! Go, Dad," I said.

"Thanks, Eric," said Dad. "Just another two to get."

Jayden groaned.

Toby looked furious and Mr Bloom didn't look too pleased, either.

"Well done, Monty," he said through gritted teeth. "Um… Toby, can I have a word?"

I watched as Mr Bloom whispered something to Toby. I was too far away to hear what they were saying but I could tell from Toby's smile that it probably wasn't good.

"What are they up to?" asked Pan.

"Not sure," I said.

Moments later Toby left his dad and headed back towards the campsite.

"Where are you off to?" I asked.

"Toilet," said Toby. "Not that it's any of your business, Crispo."

A little while later Toby returned. He was slightly out of breath and his face looked flushed. He was definitely up to something. But what?

"Hey, Monty," said Mr Bloom. "Mind if I move a bit further along the bank? I think you might have got the last fish in this part of the lake."

Dad shrugged. "Sure, no problem, Frank. If you think it'll make a difference."

Mr Bloom and Toby walked a bit further down until Toby pointed at a spot just past a large rock, and the two of them came to a stop.

A couple of minutes later Mr Bloom shouted out, **"YOU BEAUTY!"**

We all looked over as he held up his line. Dangling on the end was one of the biggest fish I've ever seen in my life.

"That's one each, Monty," yelled Mr Bloom as he handed the giant catch to Toby, before casting his reel back into the water.

Hardly a minute later, Mr Bloom called out in triumph again. "Another one, Monty! Um, what does that make it now, Toby?"

Toby scratched his head, pretending not to know. "Let's see," he shouted, holding up the two catches. "One … two. Two fish to Team Bloom. You're going down, Eric."

The second fish was even bigger than the first but it was the speed of the catch that was most surprising. What was it about that part of the lake that attracted so many fish? It didn't make any sense.

"Dad, we need to head down to where the Blooms are," I said. Dad nodded and quickly reeled in his line.

We sprinted towards the Blooms but we were too late. They were already celebrating their third catch by the time we got there, exchanging high fives before breaking out into a victory dance.

"I told you, Monty," laughed Mr Bloom. "That's pure experience at work there. Don't feel too bad, honestly. You didn't really stand a chance to begin with."

"I guess not," said Dad, scratching his head. He offered Mr Bloom his hand. "Well done, Frank."

"Thanks, Monty," said Mr Bloom, shaking it. "See that, Toby? Good sportsmanship, always important." Toby didn't look too convinced. This was the boy, after all, who would tell my mum I was cheating if I ever dared beat him at a video game.

"The winner of round one: Mr Bloom," declared Jayden.

"Congratulations, Mr Bloom," said Min. "Now, everyone, it's back to the campsite for round two."

I let the others go on in front.

"There's something fishy going on here, Pan," I said. I looked down at my right welly but Pan wasn't there. He wasn't in the left, either. "Pan? Pan, where are you?"

Moments later the head of a Mini-Dragon emerged from the lake. "They're cheating," said Pan, spitting out a jet of water.

"How?" I asked as I reached down to help him out.

"They've got a cool box full of fish down there," said Pan. "The top is open just enough to stop all the fish floating out but you could get a hook in there no problem if you knew where to lower it."

"A cool box?" I said. "Oh, of course. They had fish in their tent. So that's why Toby went off. And that's why they went further round the lake – so we wouldn't see him putting it in place. But how did they get the fish to bite if they were already dead?"

I soon found my answer. There on the ground where Mr Bloom had been "fishing" were three bits of discarded string. Toby must have tied the string round the fish, leaving a loop for the line to hook into. Then, when his dad pulled the fish out, he just threw the string away.

"You ever heard the saying, 'like shooting fish in a barrel'?" I asked.

"No," said Pan, shaking his head. "But there is a Mini-Dragon saying, 'like fishing for fish in a barrel full of fish'. I think ours is closer."

I had to give him that.

"Well, if this is how they want to do things, Pan," I said, "then four can play at that game."

CHAPTER 7
NO SMOKE WITHOUT FIRE

"Round Two has been chosen by Mr Crisp," declared Min, back at the campsite. "Building a campfire."

"The rules are simple," said Jayden. "The first person to start a fire wins. Yes, Toby?"

"Are we allowed to use matches?"

"Of course not," said Jayden.

"How about lighters?" asked Mr Bloom.

"No lighters, either," said Min. "You can use sticks and rocks, and that's it. You know, like cavemen."

Toby sneered over at us. "No phoning

your relatives for help, Eric," he said.

"Very funny, Toby," I said, unable to think of a decent comeback.

Ignoring us both, Min pressed on. "No more questions?" she said. "Good. OK—"

"Three... Two... One... Go!" interrupted Jayden.

"Hey, I wanted to do the countdown this time," said Min.

"But that's the best part," said Jayden.

As Min and Jayden bickered, Dad and Mr Bloom raced off into the forest.

Dad was back first, dumping a pile of rocks and sticks in front of me. By the time Mr Bloom showed up, Dad had his whole fire organized. A circle of carefully laid stones surrounding a tepee of sticks – thinner ones in the middle, thicker ones on the outside. This was looking much more promising. All he needed now was a spark. Taking a stick in his hands, he began whittling it against another one.

"Speaking as a Mini-Dragon," whispered Pan from my pocket, "this is the longest I've ever waited for a fire to start. Even my gran is quicker than this and she's got asthma."

After half an hour of whittling, Dad was no closer to getting a fire going than when he'd begun. Mr Bloom, meanwhile, had spent the time bashing two rocks together with just as much success.

"You have done this before, right, Dad?" I asked.

"Sure, plenty of times," said Dad. "Well, I suppose if you want to get technical, it was your grandad really. But I must have *watched* him do it a dozen times."

"Oh," I said. "And did it normally take

him this long?"

"Well, no…" admitted Dad. "Although I think wood was different in those days."

Jayden was close to falling asleep again and Min was still leafing through the guidebook. Pan and I were watching the Blooms like hawks, waiting for them to try something else.

"Er … how's it going with you, Monty?" asked Mr Bloom.

"Nothing yet, Frank," admitted Dad. "Any second now, though, I think."

"Yeah, me, too," said Mr Bloom. But it was obvious from the look on his face that he didn't really believe that. "Toby, could you come here a second?"

Mr Bloom whispered something into his son's ear. Toby nodded and headed back towards their tent.

"Where's he going?" asked Pan.

"Probably off to get matches or a firelighter," I said. "It wouldn't surprise me if that tent came with a flamethrower. It's got everything else."

And then I remembered. We actually *did* have a flamethrower. A fifteen-centimetre tall one. The rules said no matches or lighters. They didn't say anything about

Mini-Dragons.

"Pan," I said. "You have to help my dad win before Toby gets back."

"You mean ... cheat?" asked Pan.

"If we don't then they will," I said. "They already have, remember?"

Pan still didn't look too sure and, even as I said it, I realized I wasn't sure, either. If Dad lost the contest, I was pretty sure Frank Bloom would never let him live it down. And it didn't seem right to stand by and let the Blooms cheat their way to victory. On the other hand, if *we* cheated, wouldn't that make us just as bad?

Of course it would. Two wrongs don't make a right. I was about to tell Pan to forget it when a small red spark left his mouth and landed in the middle of Dad's pile of sticks. Suddenly, the whole thing burst into flames. Dad jumped back in surprise.

"I did it!" he shouted, throwing his arms in the air in celebration.

I glanced over at Mr Bloom, who did not look happy. Then Toby reappeared from the tent. When he looked our way his face turned so red it probably could have started a fire itself. And there in his hand was a…

…bottle of water. No matches, no lighter and definitely no flamethrower. He had gone to get his dad a drink.

"Mr Crisp ties the score," said Jayden.

"Not too bad, eh, Eric?" beamed Dad.

"Er… Nice one, Dad," I said. I felt horrible. I'd wanted him to win but not like this. At least there was one more challenge to go. Dad could still win that fair and square.

My eyes drifted to the judges – to Min in particular. Her eyes locked on to mine. It was like they were boring a hole right through my head. She was not happy. She knew.

CHAPTER 8

CAUGHT IN THE ACT

"I saw what you did," said Min once we were out of earshot of Dad and the Blooms. I had never seen her look so angry.

"Min … I … er … that is…" I stammered, trying to find the right words to diffuse the Min-shaped bomb that was about to go off.

"What did he do?" asked Jayden.

"Both of them," said Min, eyeballing Pan as he peered nervously out of my pocket. "They cheated. Pan started that fire, not Mr Crisp. And I saw the way you were acting beforehand, Eric. I know that it was all your idea."

Jayden stared at her in disbelief. "Eric? Cheating?" he said. "Come on, Min, you don't seriously believe that, do you?"

"She's right," I said quietly. "We cheated. I asked Pan to do it."

Jayden was stunned. "Not cool, mate," he said. "Not cool."

"I know," I said. "I'm sorry. I did change my mind but it was too late. Anyway, we only did it because we found out that Toby and his dad cheated in the fishing contest."

"It's true," said Pan. "I found a cool box of fish in the lake."

Min shook her head. "So why didn't you just come and tell us?" she said. "We could have had them disqualified."

"Well, because..." I said, before stopping. I looked down at Pan. "Actually, why *didn't* we do that?"

"Yeah, that would have been a much better idea," agreed Pan.

I had been so mad at the Blooms that I hadn't been thinking clearly. I'd just wanted to get even.

"And you, Pan," said Min, turning her attention towards the quivering Mini-Dragon. "How could you have agreed to it? What would your mum think?"

"I'm sorry," said Pan sheepishly. "You're not going to tell her, are you?"

Min seemed to be considering it for a moment, then her face softened. "No, probably not," she said. "But it's the sort of thing you'd expect from your aunt and uncle, not from you."

Pan and I hung our heads in shame.

"So what are we going to do then?" asked Jayden. "Disqualify them?"

Min frowned. "No," she said. "We can't. How could we do that without telling everyone about Pan?"

Min looked down at the guidebook in her hands and a mischievous smile crept across her face. "No..." she said. "We're not going to disqualify you. The opposite, in fact. Since you and Toby want to help your dads win so much, I think I might have the perfect challenge..."

"I don't understand," said Toby with a blank face once Min had finished explaining the final challenge.

Min sighed. "Look, it's all written here," she said, pointing to a page in the guidebook.

The Lost Tooth of Lake Cress

IN 1899, the fabulously wealthy, but notoriously dim, Charles Babblington, Third Duke of Cress, got into a fist fight with a grizzly bear after the animal didn't take kindly to being told it wasn't native to England.

The Duke lost the fight in the end – of course he did, he was fighting a bear – but he did live to tell the tale. Also lost in the battle was the Duke's diamond-encrusted gold canine tooth. The Duke would spend the rest of his life searching the woods for his missing tooth but to no avail.

Over the years the search has been taken up by visitors to Lake Cress, a tradition that continues to this day. Will you be the one to finally find the Duke's tooth? Watch out for those bears, though!

[Disclaimer – Our lawyers have asked us to point out that there are definitely no bears in the Lake Cress area.]

Toby looked at Min, his expression unchanged. "OK, I get all that," he said. "I just don't understand what it has to do with me."

"As this is the final round," said Min, "we're making it a father and son challenge."

"You mean I'd be out there, in the woods?" asked Toby. "Walking? You've got to be kidding."

"That's right, Toby." Min folded her arms. "Are you saying you forfeit?"

"What! No, I never said that," said Toby, looking to me for help. For once I was on his side, although for different reasons.

"You're sending us out to look for a tooth?" I said. "You can't be serious."

"I think she's pretty serious," said Jayden.

"Come on, Eric," said Dad. "It could be fun…"

"Yeah, but even if this story is real," I said, "and if it's anything like all those other legends then I doubt it is, no one's found this thing in over a hundred years. What are the chances of any of us finding it? It's impossible."

Mr Bloom gave Toby a nudge. "What do you think, Toby?" he said. "Sounds to me like Eric's trying to get himself a draw."

A look of determination mixed with scorn filled Toby's face. "I agree," he said. "But then you've always been a quitter, Crispo. You might not be up for the challenge but we are. In fact, the only reason that dumb tooth is still out there is because no Bloom ever went looking for it. Let's go, Dad."

Before I could open my mouth, Toby and his dad were off, disappearing into the woods.

"Hang on," moaned Min. "I was supposed to shout 'Three-two-one-go'. Oh, forget it."

Dad turned to face me. "What do you

say, Eric?" he asked. "Is Team Crisp up for the challenge?"

As long as the Blooms were out there they had a shot of winning. We couldn't let that happen.

I nodded.

"Great," said Dad. He looked at Min and Jayden. "Will you two be all right on your own? You're welcome to come."

"We'll be fine," Min said. "Plus, we need to be here in case Toby and his dad get back first with the tooth."

"They won't," I said. I patted the pocket of my jeans. "But I've got my walkie-talkie if you need to reach us."

"Good thinking, Eric," said Dad. He glanced in the direction the Blooms had run off in. "Probably would have been an idea if they had taken one, too. Oh well, I'm sure they can look after themselves. Now, what are we waiting for?"

We had only taken a few steps when Min shouted after me.

"I'll catch up," I said to Dad as I headed back. "What's wrong?"

"Pan stays here," she said.

"What?" said Pan. "Why?"

"No more Mini-Dragon assistance," she said firmly. "You can stay here with us.

Jayden and I can help you practise your flying while we wait."

Pan looked up at me but all I could offer was a shrug. "Sorry," I said.

"Come on, Pan. It's got to be better than traipsing around a forest looking for some dead guy's tooth," said Jayden.

"You've obviously never seen me fly," said Pan.

CHAPTER 9

THE TOOTH COMES OUT

"What about this?" I said, holding up a tiny yellowish object.

Dad squinted at it for a second before shaking his head. "That's just a stone."

I tossed it away and picked up a smaller, darker item. "This maybe?" I asked, giving it a sniff. It smelled gross but then I supposed a hundred-year-old tooth was bound to smell a bit iffy, even if it was made of gold.

"Er … no, Eric, that's a bit of rabbit poo."

"EURGH!" I shouted, flinging the pellet into the trees.

We had been trekking through the forest for hours. I was tired and hungry, and we were no closer to finding the tooth than when we'd started. But I didn't care about that. We had to beat the Blooms. Nothing else mattered.

And it hadn't been *all* bad. Dad had been telling me loads of stories from when he used to go camping, like the time my grandad went for a wee and it had been so windy that their tent had blown away, with Dad still in it.

"This is nice, eh?" Dad said. "Just you and me out in the wilderness."

"Yeah," I agreed. "I just wish we could find that tooth."

Dad smiled. "You know, I remember the legend from when I was young," he said. "The place used to be packed with people searching for that thing. Those stories don't seem to be working any more, though. Ah well, I guess we should think about calling it a day. It'll be dark soon."

I looked up at the sky. He was right, the light was already beginning to fade.

"We can't go back yet," I said. "Not without the tooth."

Dad laughed. "It's just a tooth, Eric," he said. "A tooth that probably doesn't even exist."

"But if we don't find it we won't win the challenge," I said.

Dad shrugged. "Would that be so bad?"

"Of course!" I said. "We can't lose to the Blooms."

Dad nodded. I thought for a second that he was agreeing with me but then he sat down on a rock and motioned for me to sit next to him.

"Eric, do you ever wonder why I still do my job?" he asked.

"I suppose it has crossed my mind..." I said, remembering that the Kippers had only ever won two games in their entire history.

"Because I love football," he said. "I love watching it, I love playing it, I love everything about it. All I ever wanted when I grew up was to be around football. My job lets me do that. And I get to hang out with a great group of lads who feel the same way. None of us is very good but every one of us loves the game. Do you get what I'm saying?"

I thought about it for a few moments. "Sorry, Dad," I said. "I haven't got a clue what you're on about."

"My point is that winning is nice but it's not the be all and end all," he said. "The Kippers enjoy themselves every week, come rain or shine. And this weekend … it wasn't meant to be about competing with our neighbours. It was about us all having a good time, like I did when your grandad used to bring me here. Have you been having a good time, Eric?"

I had enjoyed parts of the last couple of hours spent with Dad but overall? "No," I admitted. "But maybe if we can just find the tooth…"

"…that might not even exist," said Dad.

I sighed. "We've wasted the whole weekend, haven't we?"

"Not the whole weekend," he said.

"We still have tonight and tomorrow."

"That's if we can find our way back to camp," I said.

We started walking back up the path when a thought occurred to me. "Dad, why did you agree to the contest in the first place?" I asked.

Dad shrugged. "I don't know," he said. "You seemed to want me to do it. And I'll admit, the thought of beating Frank was quite appealing. Although I think it's obvious by now that I'm not quite the outdoorsman that my dad is. I won't grumble too much – at least I've got to hang out with my son."

I smiled. "Yeah, I've liked that part, too." I took my walkie-talkie out of my pocket and clicked the talk button. "Hey, Min, Jayden, we're on our way back now. Everything all right? Are the Blooms there?"

There was silence on the other end. Just as

I was starting to worry, I heard a crackle then Jayden say: "Oh, hey, Eric. Yep… Nope, no Blooms yet… Everything's great here… Yep, no problems… Uh … see you soon…"

I thought Jayden sounded a little on edge. I was about to mention it to Dad when he came to an abrupt stop at the top of the hill and let out a gasp. "Eric, look," he said, pointing ahead of him.

For a moment I thought he might have actually spotted the tooth but as I looked up I saw something much better. The sun was setting over Lake Cress, lighting up the water in a blazing mix of oranges, reds and yellows.

"Wow," I said.

"Wow indeed," said Dad.

"I'm glad we're done with this stupid competition," I said as we sat down on a log to take in the view. "But it still would have been kind of nice to win. I guess I could live with a draw, though."

"I wouldn't count on it," said Dad. "After the fishing challenge, I wouldn't put it past them to knock out one of their own teeth and paint it gold."

The thought made me burst into laughter. Then what Dad had just said hit me. "Wait … you know that they cheated?"

"Of course," said Dad, smiling. "I half expected them to catch a box of fish fingers the way they were going."

I couldn't believe it. "Why didn't you say something?" I asked.

"Well, I didn't want to embarrass them," said Dad. "I don't know if you've noticed but winning is quite important to the Blooms."

"Yeah, I had noticed that actually," I said. It was time to come clean. "Dad ... while we're on the subject ... you might not have won your challenge completely fairly, either."

It wasn't that easy to see in the forest now but even in the dark I could make out the look of disappointment on Dad's face.

"Eric ... how?" he said, before shaking his head. "No, don't bother telling me. I don't want to know. Just promise me that you'll never stoop to anything like that again."

"I promise, Dad," I said, staring at the ground.

"Good," he said. "I'd expect that from Toby. And it's one thing living next door to a boy like that but I'd rather not have to live with one, too." Dad paused. "Seriously, can you imagine *that?*"

We both shuddered at the thought.

Thankfully it didn't take us very long to return to camp, probably because we weren't stopping every few metres to examine animal droppings. As the last of the light faded, Dad used the torch on his key ring to lead us the rest of the way. With my feet killing me and my stomach rumbling, I was glad to be back.

Until I saw our tent.

Or what was left of it.

CHAPTER 10

THE IMPORTANCE OF PANTS

Our tent lay in pieces. Ropes were snapped, poles were broken and the canvas was full of holes.

Min and Jayden were standing next to the heap, gazing at us wide-eyed in a mixture of panic and embarrassment.

"What happened?" said Dad, looking stunned. "Are you both OK?"

Min and Jayden nodded. "We're fine, Mr Crisp," said Min. "We were … uh … racing each other and … uh…"

"…didn't see the tent," continued Jayden.

"What, did it sneak up on you?" asked Dad.

Min and Jayden laughed nervously. "Something like that," said Min.

"Oh well," said Dad, trying his best to put on a brave face. "Accidents happen."

"Sorry, Mr Crisp," they said quietly.

"I guess I'd better get our stuff out," said Dad. "We'll have to sleep in Castle Bloom tonight."

As Dad began to rummage through the wreckage, I looked at Min and Jayden. Slowly the head of a very guilty-looking Mini-Dragon emerged from Min's welly.

"And to think you told me off for lying," I whispered to Min.

"I told you off for cheating," corrected Min.

"Same difference," I said. "What happened?"

"Pan's flying practice didn't go very well," said Jayden.

I gazed down at Pan. He looked miserable.

"It's all right, Pan," I said. "You'll get the hang of it eventually. I know you will."

Pan shook his head. "You didn't see me," he muttered. "I was out of control."

I was about to reach down and comfort him when Dad reappeared from the tent.

"Eric, why were these taped to your sleeping compartment," he asked, holding up my pants.

Min and Jayden exploded with laughter as I snatched them out of his hands.

"I ... er ... they're the pair I had on when I went swimming," I fibbed, stuffing my pants into my pocket.

"Oh," said Dad. "Well, they seem dry now. No sign of Toby and Frank?"

"No, not yet," said Jayden.

"Hmm," said Dad. "They must really want to win. It's way past dinner time now, and it's not like either of them to skip a meal. Speaking of which, I'll make us some salami sandwiches while we wait. Maybe the smell will entice them back."

It didn't. An hour after we had finished our sandwiches (and Pan had finished his prawn crackers), there was still no sign of the Blooms.

"What if something's gone wrong?" I said, immediately picturing things that might have happened to Toby and his dad:

- They were lost.

- They'd been kidnapped.

- They'd been eaten.

- They'd fallen into the lake.

- They'd stumbled across a Chick-a-Licious Express in the woods.

- They'd found a portal to another dimension.

They'd accidentally disturbed the grave of the bear that fought the Duke of Cress, angering its ghost.

I shook my head. It probably wasn't the ghost bear or the portal. But they could easily be lost.

"You three stay here," said Dad. "I'm going to the phone box to call the emergency services."

"Pan," I said, once the beam of Dad's torch was out of sight. "We need your help."

Pan screwed up his face. "Me?"

"It might take the emergency services all night to search the woods but if you were to fly..." I said.

He looked at me like he had just seen a ghost bear. "Have you not seen what I did to the tent?" he asked.

"Don't worry about that," I said. "You can do this, Pan, I know you can. You're the best hope we have of finding them." Even though all of Pan's flying attempts had ended in disaster, somehow I still believed what I was saying. Mini-Dragons were excellent at coming through in a crisis.

"How's he going to see in the dark?" asked Jayden.

"Haven't you read the *Encyclopaedia Dragonica*?" Min said, giving him a withering look.

The *Encyclopaedia Dragonica* is the ultimate guide to all things dragon – Mini and otherwise.

"It's, er … on my reading list," said Jayden. "Haven't got round to it yet, that's all. What does it say?"

Min nipped into Castle Bloom and returned with the giant book.

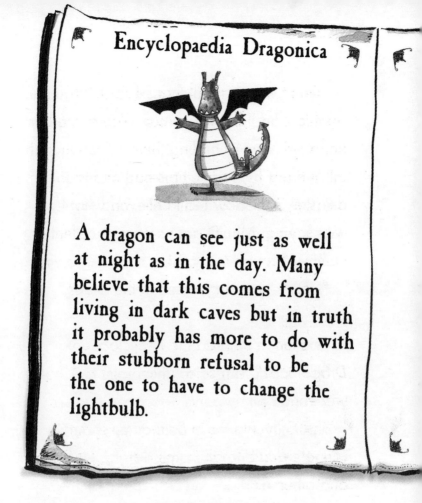

Encyclopaedia Dragonica

A dragon can see just as well at night as in the day. Many believe that this comes from living in dark caves but in truth it probably has more to do with their stubborn refusal to be the one to have to change the lightbulb.

Pan frowned. "Seeing in the dark isn't the problem," he said. "It's the getting off the ground part that's the issue. I have to concentrate so hard on actually getting into the air that when I finally manage it, I forget what I'm supposed to do next."

I scratched my head for a moment, trying to think of a solution.

"I've got it," I said. I took my pants out of my pocket, and turned to Min and Jayden. "Grab an end each."

"Eww!" said Min, pulling her hand away.

"Dude, I am not touching your pants," said Jayden.

"Just do it," I said.

Still looking disgusted, they each took hold of a corner of my pants. I scooped Pan up and put him into the middle of my underwear. Then I pulled back the pants, stretching them as far as they'd go and aiming Pan at the sky.

"You've made a slingshot," said Jayden, looking both horrified and impressed.

"The Pan Pants Express," I said. "You ready, Pan?"

"Not really," he said.

"Remember, steady flapping, nice and smooth," I said.

"Actually, Eric, can we talk about this for a—"

It was at that point that my fingers slipped. *Honest.*

Pan was flung into the night sky. For a second we saw a tiny silhouette of a dragon against the moon, then he was gone.

"Well, I hope that worked," said Min.

"Yeah, or we may have just squished Pan," said Jayden.

CHAPTER 11
THE HOLE TRUTH

Around five minutes later Pan reappeared.
The three of us breathed a huge sigh of relief
as we watched him begin to descend. Then
we realized that instead of slowing down,
he was speeding up. We scrambled to try
and catch him but Pan shot past us like a
meteorite, landing head first on the ground.

I scooped him up. "Pan, are you OK?"

He blinked a couple of times. "Told you...
Tough ... are ... Mini-Dragons..." he said.

"Did you see them?" asked Min.

A groggy-looking Pan gave a brief nod.
"Ten to fifteen minutes away... just off ... path
near lake... Toby's dad ... stuck in a hole."

"A hole?" I said. "How'd he do that?"

Pan shrugged as his eyes finally seemed
to focus. "Well, I didn't exactly stop to
ask."

"Fair point. Well done, Pan," I said. "I
knew you wouldn't let us down."

Pan stuck out his tiny chest. "I was pretty
amazing, wasn't I? I might even have a
future in the Mini-Dragon stunt-flying team –
the Red Dragons."

"You'll need to work on your landing
first," Min pointed out.

"And you did need a pair of pants to take

off," noted Jayden.

Pan looked at them, stony-faced. "Honestly, can't you just let me have this moment?" he asked.

Min and Jayden's faces turned red. "Sorry, Pan," they said.

"There's your dad," said Jayden, pointing to a torch beam approaching us.

Pan slipped down into my welly as Dad came into view. "The phone's out," he said.

"We'll have to go and find them ourselves then," I said.

"Absolutely not," said Dad. "I'll take the car and drive to the other campsite, speak to the site manager."

"But I know where they are," I said.

This got me a funny look from Dad. "How could you possibly know that?" he asked.

"They ... they were heading towards the lake," I said, trying to sound as confident as

I could. "There's a trail that runs alongside it. I walked down it this morning when I went for a swim, they'd have seen it, too. You know the Blooms – they always take the easy path."

Dad stroked his beard thoughtfully, not looking entirely convinced.

"We can't just leave them out there," I said.

"As tempting as that might be," put in Jayden, "Eric's right, we've got to go and look for them."

"They'd do the same for us," added Min, before realizing her mistake. "Sorry, what am I saying? Of course they wouldn't. But that doesn't mean we shouldn't."

"All right," Dad said. "Everyone grab a torch. Let's go."

"TOBY!!!"

"MR BLOOM!!!"

With Pan tucked into the hood of my jacket, we followed the path near the lake by torchlight, yelling out to the Blooms as we went. But all we could hear in return was the sound of our own footsteps. Until –

"CRISPO? IS THAT YOU? WE'RE OVER HERE!"

All the torch beams swung in the same direction, momentarily blinding Toby.

"Gah! Turn those off," he moaned as we all rushed over.

"Toby," said Dad. "Thank goodness you're OK. Where's your dad?"

"Down here," came a sheepish voice.

We all turned our torch beams in the direction of the voice. There, in a deep hole in the ground, was Mr Bloom.

"Frank! What happened?" asked Dad.

There was a loud sigh from the hole. "Honestly, Monty, what do you think happened?" said Mr Bloom. "We were looking for that stupid tooth and I didn't see this huge hole. So unless you have any more questions, would you mind **GETTING ME OUT OF HERE?**"

"Is he hurt?" asked Min.

"Just his pride," muttered Dad. "Now, how are we going to get him out, I wonder?"

"I tried to pull him out with a stick," said

Toby, pointing towards a large pile of branches lying nearby. "But I couldn't find one long enough to reach."

Dad looked at the heap thoughtfully.

"Eric," he said, "have you still got your underpants?"

"His *what*?" asked Toby.

I had an idea about where Dad might be going with this. I reached into my pocket for the pants hammock/catapult and handed it over. Dad wrapped the pants around two bits of wood, tying them together to make a super long stick.

We all grabbed on to one end and lowered it into the hole. With Mr Bloom gripping the other end, we began to pull him out. But just as we were about to heave him over the top, he let out a huge scream.

"Something bit me on the bum!" he shouted as we dragged him out.

Dad shone his torch on to Mr Bloom's
backside. There, lodged into his trousers,
was a single, sharp-looking golden tooth
with a tiny diamond sparkling in the middle.

Dad's mouth opened and closed a few times. "Some tooth-hunter probably dug that hole and had no idea how close they came to finding it. Hmm … the tooth looks like it's stuck in there pretty tight, Frank. Let me check my first-aid kit for a pair of tweezers…"

But that wasn't necessary. In one swift motion, Toby reached down and yanked the tooth out.

"Look, Dad, we did it. We beat the Crisps!" he said, holding up his glittering prize.

Mr Bloom's response probably wasn't the one Toby was looking for.

"AAAAARRGGHHHHHH!"

CHAPTER 12

THE LEGEND OF THE LAKE CRESS MONSTER

By the time we helped Mr Bloom hobble back to camp, we were all ready for bed. Except for the Blooms who stayed up celebrating, eating victory sandwiches.

Since our tent was destroyed, Dad and I had to spend the night in Castle Bloom. At least it meant I got a good night's sleep. The room dividers were thick enough to block out Dad's snores. Of course, I still had Pan's to deal with but in the end I came up with a great solution. I've written a handy guide here:

How To Cope with a Snoring Mini-Dragon

You will need: 2 pairs of pants
(briefs recommended,
but any will do)

Instructions:

Step 1: Roll up one pair and place
the end of it in your left ear.
If necessary, fix in place with
medical tape.

Step 2: Repeat for right ear.

Step 3: Sleep.

The following day, we went fishing after breakfast and, amazingly, everyone caught something, although nothing was as big as the fish from the cool box.

We went swimming in the lake. We climbed trees. We had a barbecue. And we played all sorts of games – volleyball, football, badminton, Frisbee – Castle Bloom had all the gear we needed.

Even the Blooms got involved, though I think that might have had something to do with Mr Bloom having a hard time sitting down. Even so they actually seemed to enjoy themselves. They were much more tolerable when they weren't being quite so Bloom-ish. Obviously they spent most of the time bragging about winning the competition and talking about making the Bloom-Crisp Games an annual event but that's only to be expected. They weren't so keen when Dad suggested that they donate the tooth to a museum.

I realized, though, that in their own weird way, Mr Bloom and Toby were just like me and my dad. They had both wanted to spend the weekend hanging out with each other. Their idea of a fun camping holiday was rather different to mine but that didn't give me any right to ruin their enjoyment. So I asked Pan if there was any way to turn the power back on. Of course, wouldn't you know it, Mini-Dragons are excellent at fixing generators.

Other than that, I didn't see too much of Pan that day. He was busy getting used to his wings, exploring Lake Cress via the skies. He still needed the help of my pants to get airborne and his landings were as hard to watch as ever but he was getting there.

That night we brought the TV outside and

watched movies under the stars. After a bit Pan and I left the others watching Slug Man again and sat down next to the campfire. With everyone looking away from us and the TV volume turned way up, we put marshmallows on to sticks and toasted them in the fire. Well, actually Pan just toasted his himself. And even though marshmallows aren't part of the three dragon food groups, he seemed to enjoy them.

"I can't believe we've made it through a whole weekend without either of the Blooms even coming close to spotting you," I said.

"I told you before that it wouldn't be a problem," said Pan. "Mini-Dragons are excellent at keeping out of sight."

That hadn't exactly been my experience so far but I didn't bother to argue.

After finishing off yet another gooey marshmallow, I decided to ask Pan about something that had been worrying me since he learned how to fly. "Do you think your parents might want you to go back and live with them?" I said. "I mean, it'd be safe for you to live up in the mountains now."

Pan shook his head. "Once a Mini-Dragon learns to fly, the rule is that it's up to him where he lives," he replied. "And I want to live with you. If that's still all right?"

I smiled. "Of course it is!"

Pan smiled, too. A few seconds passed. "Actually," he said, "have I remembered that right? Maybe I just made that rule up. On second thoughts, it's probably safer if we just don't tell them anything."

I laughed. "No problem," I said.

"Besides," added Pan, "I don't think Mum and Dad will be too impressed if I were to show up still needing a pair of pants to take off."

"Probably not," I agreed.

Pan looked at the fire then turned towards me. "How about it?" he said. "Just once?"

"OK," I said, getting to my feet and stepping back. "Just this once."

Pan turned round, counted to three then let out a massive fart right into the fire, sending a huge ball of flames into the air.

Pan opted to fly home the following morning, rather than ride with us in the car. But as we left the campsite something strange seemed to be going on. The site now had a long queue of cars trying to get in. We must have driven past hundreds on the road out.

"That's odd," said Dad. "I wonder if news about the tooth has spread already? Not sure why they're bothering to come now, though. It's not like there are more to be found. Still, nice to see business picking up."

I spent the rest of the journey home trying to figure out how the Blooms had possibly got word out so fast. I still couldn't explain it by the time we stepped through the front door.

"Welcome back," said Mum, hugging us as we came in. Posy appeared, too, throwing her arms round our legs. Pusskin, meanwhile, took one look at us, sniffed and turned away.

"How was your weekend?" asked Dad.

"I slept so well," said Mum. "It was nice not to have to put up with your snoring for a few nights."

Dad looked hurt. "I don't snore, do I, Eric?" he asked.

"HA!" I blurted out.

Dad scowled at me. "Hmm ... anything interesting happen here?"

"Wait till you hear all our stories," said Mum. "Although I'm sure they won't be half as exciting as yours. It's all over the news. Did you actually see it?"

"Of course we did," said Dad. "We were the ones that found it."

Mum's eyes bulged. "Really? Were you scared?"

"Er … no," said Dad, looking confused. "I mean … it was slightly gross but our goalkeeper has worse ones."

This time it was Mum who looked confused. "Your … goalkeeper? Are we talking about the same thing?"

"Well, what are you talking about?" asked Dad.

"The monster," said Mum.

Dad and I looked at each other.

"He's called Toby, Mum," I said.

"Yeah, you shouldn't call him that, love," said Dad.

"What?" she said. "No, not Toby! Are you serious? Have you not seen the picture?"

"What picture?" asked Dad.

Mum rushed through to the living room and appeared moments later with a newspaper. "Look," she said, pressing it against Dad's chest.

We both read the headline:

BEAST SPOTTED IN LAKE CRESS

Beneath that was a very grainy picture of the head of some creature emerging from the water. It looked like a big monster shot from a distance. But I knew it wasn't. It was a little monster, shot from close up.

I stared at it in disbelief. And then I remembered. That first morning out on the lake. But who could have taken the photo? There was no one there but us. Except…

The people in the other campsite.

If the picture had been taken a few seconds later, it probably would have shown an out-of-breath, freezing boy swimming towards the monster.

"Well, it looks like they've found a new legend," laughed Dad.

Then I remembered something else. I bolted up the stairs and into my bedroom, just in time to open my window. A tiny green creature hurtled through the gap, splatting into my wall and sliding to the floor in a crumpled heap.

There, smiling up at me with a dazed look on his face, was the Lake Cress Monster.

ABOUT THE AUTHOR

Tom Nicoll has been writing since he was at school, where he enjoyed trying to fit in as much silliness to his essays as he could possibly get away with. When not writing, he enjoys playing video games (especially the ones where he gets beaten by kids half his age from all over the world). He is also a big comedy, TV and movie nerd. Tom lives just outside Edinburgh with his wife, daughter and a cat that thinks it's a dog.

THERE'S A DRAGON IN MY PANTS!
is his fourth book for children.

ABOUT THE ILLUSTRATOR

Sarah Horne grew up in Derbyshire and spent much of her childhood scampering in the nearby fields with a few goats. Then she decided to be sensible and studied Illustration at Falmouth College of Arts and gained a Master's degree at Kingston University.

She now lives in London and specializes in funny, inky illustration.

COLLECT THEM ALL!

KE 3/17

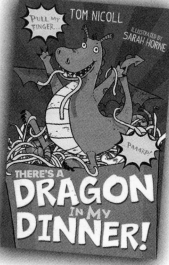